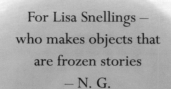

For Lisa Snellings —
who makes objects that
are frozen stories
— N. G.

For my Uma kutty
and her Ammamma and Thatha —
I love you.
— D. S.

Cinnamon was a princess, a long time ago, in a small hot country, where everything was very old.

Cinnamon

NEIL GAIMAN

Illustrated by DIVYA SRINIVASAN

BLOOMSBURY
CHILDREN'S BOOKS
LONDON OXFORD NEW YORK NEW DELHI SYDNEY

BLOOMSBURY CHILDREN'S BOOKS
Bloomsbury Publishing Plc
50 Bedford Square, London WC1B 3DP, UK

BLOOMSBURY, BLOOMSBURY CHILDREN'S BOOKS and the Diana logo
are trademarks of Bloomsbury Publishing Plc

First published in Great Britain in 2017 by Bloomsbury Publishing Plc
This edition published in Great Britain in 2019 by Bloomsbury Publishing Plc

A catalogue record for this book is available from the British Library

ISBN: HB: 978 1 4088 7923 8; PB: 978 1 4088 7922 1; eBook: 978 1 4088 7921 4

2 4 6 8 10 9 7 5 3 1

Printed in China by Leo Paper Products, Heshan, Guangdong

All papers used by Bloomsbury Publishing Plc are natural, recyclable products from wood grown in well managed forests. The
manufacturing processes conform to the environmental regulations of the country of origin

To find out more about our authors and books visit www.bloomsbury.com
and sign up for our newsletters

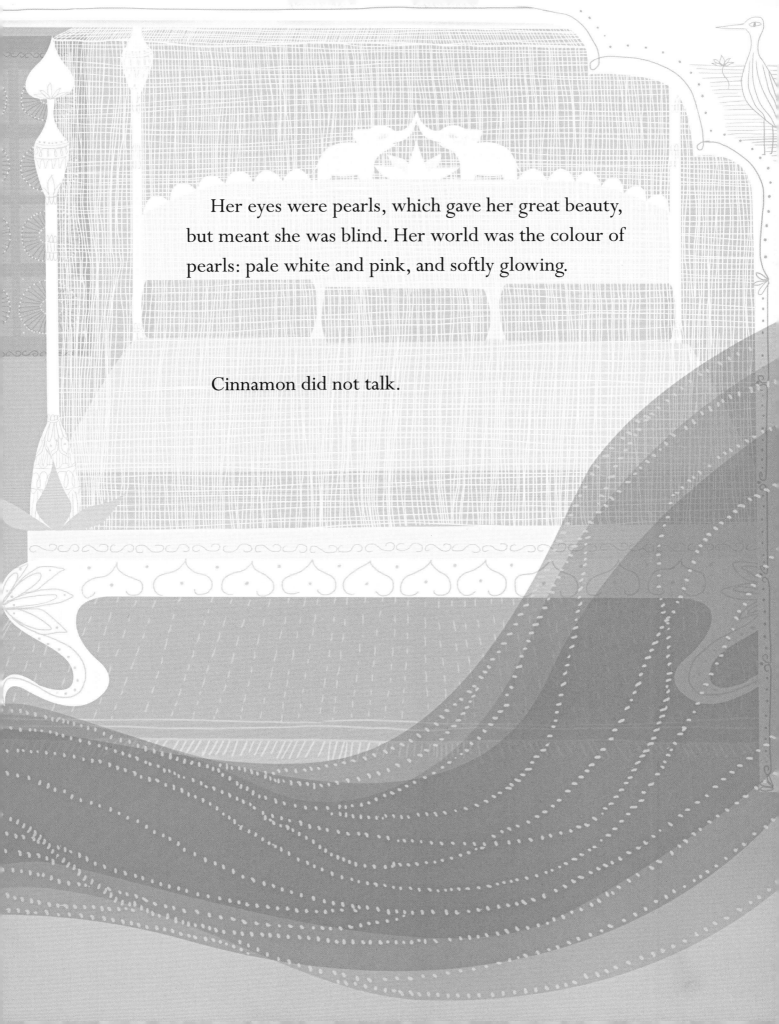

Her eyes were pearls, which gave her great beauty, but meant she was blind. Her world was the colour of pearls: pale white and pink, and softly glowing.

Cinnamon did not talk.

Her father and her mother – the Rajah and the Rani – offered a room in the palace, a field of stunted mango trees, a portrait of the Rani's aunt executed on hardwood in enamels and a green parrot, to any person who could get Cinnamon to talk.

The mountains ringed the country on one side, the jungle on the other; and few and far came the people to try to teach Cinnamon to speak.

But come they did: and they stayed in the room in the palace, and cultivated the field of mango trees,

and fed the parrot, and admired the portrait of the Rani's aunt (who was quite a celebrated beauty in her day, although she was now old and crabbed and pinched with age and disappointment),

and, eventually, they went
away, frustrated, and cursing
the silent little girl.

One day a tiger came to the palace. He was huge and fierce, a nightmare in black and orange, and he moved like a god through the world, which is how tigers move. The people were afraid.

"There is nothing to be frightened of," said the Rajah. "Very few tigers are man-eaters."

"But I am," said the tiger.

The people were much amazed that the tiger could speak, although it did nothing whatsoever to quell their fear.

"You might be lying," said the Rajah.
"I might be," said the tiger. "But I'm not. Now: I am here to teach the girl-cub to talk."

The Rajah consulted with the Rani, and, despite the urgings of the Rani's aunt, who was of the opinion that the tiger should be driven out from the city with brooms and sharp sticks, the tiger was shown to the room in the palace, and given the enamel painting, and the deeds to the mango field, and he would also have been given the parrot, had it not squawked and flown to the rafters, where it stayed and refused to come down.

Cinnamon was shown into the tiger's room.

"*There was a young lady from Riga,*" squawked the parrot, from high in the rafters, "*who went for a ride on a tiger.*

"*They came back from the ride with the lady inside and a smile on the face of the tiger.*"

(Although, in the interests of historical and literary accuracy, I am obliged to point out here that the parrot actually quoted another poem, much older, and a little longer, with, ultimately, a similar message.)

"There," said the Rani's
aunt. "Even the bird knows."
"Leave me with the girl,"
said the tiger.

And, reluctantly, the Rajah and the Rani and the Rani's aunt and the palace staff left the beast with Cinnamon. She pushed her fingers into its fur, and felt its hot breath on her face.

The tiger put Cinnamon's hand into his.

"Pain," said the tiger, and he extended one needle-sharp claw into Cinnamon's hand. It pierced her soft brown skin, and a bead of bright blood welled up.

Cinnamon whimpered.

"Fear," said the tiger, and he began to roar, starting so quietly you could scarcely hear it, working his way up to a purr, then a quiet roar, like a distant volcano, then to a roar so loud that the palace walls shook.

Cinnamon trembled.

"Love," said the tiger, and with his rough red tongue he licked the blood from Cinnamon's hand, and licked her soft brown face.

"Love?" whispered Cinnamon, in a voice wild and dark from disuse.

And the tiger opened his mouth and grinned like a hungry god, which is how tigers grin.

The moon was full that night.

It was bright morning when the child and the tiger walked out of the room together. Cymbals crashed, and bright birds sang, and Cinnamon and the tiger walked towards the Rani and the Rajah, who sat at one end of the throne room, being fanned with palm fronds by elderly retainers.

The Rani's aunt sat in a corner of the room, drinking tea disapprovingly.

"Can she talk yet?" asked the Rani.

"Why don't you ask her?" growled the tiger.

"Can you talk?" the Rajah asked Cinnamon.

The girl nodded.

"Hah!" cackled the Rani's aunt. "She can no more talk than she can lick her own backbone!"

"Hush," said the Rajah to the Rani's aunt.

"I can talk," said Cinnamon. "I think I always could."

"Then why didn't you?" asked her mother.

"She's not talking now," muttered the Rani's aunt, wagging one sticklike finger. "That tiger is throwing his voice."

"Can no one get that woman to stop talking?" asked the Rajah of the room.

"Easier to stop 'em than start 'em," said the tiger, and he dealt with the matter.

And Cinnamon said, "Why not? Because I
had nothing to say."
"And now?" asked her father.

"And now the tiger has told me of the jungle, of the
chattering of the monkeys and the smell of the dawn and the
taste of the moonlight and the noise a lakeful of flamingos makes
when it takes to the air," she said. "And what I have to say is this:
I am going with the tiger."
"You cannot do this thing," said the Rajah. "I forbid it."

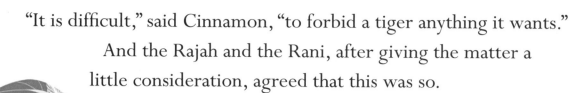

"It is difficult," said Cinnamon, "to forbid a tiger anything it wants."
And the Rajah and the Rani, after giving the matter a
little consideration, agreed that this was so.

"And besides," said the Rani, "she'll
certainly be happier there."

"But what about the room in the palace? And the mango grove? And the parrot? And the picture of the Rani's late aunt?" asked the Rajah, who felt that there was a place for practicality in the world.

"Give them to the people," said the tiger.

And so an announcement was made to the people of the city that they were now the proud owners of a parrot, a portrait, and a mango grove, and that the Princess Cinnamon could speak, but would be leaving them for a while to further her education.

A crowd gathered in the town square, and soon the door of the
palace opened, and the tiger and the child came out. The tiger walked
slowly through the crowd with the little girl on his back, holding
tightly to his fur, and soon they both were swallowed by the jungle.

So, in the end, nobody was eaten, save only the Rani's elderly aunt, who was gradually replaced in the popular mind by the portrait of her, which hung in the town square, and was thus forever beautiful and young.